BLUE Sky YELLOW Kite

Janet A. Holmes & Jonathan Bentley

Peter Pauper Press, Inc.
WHITE PLAINS, NEW YORK

Blue sky, yellow kite.

The kite flits, darts, and flies, tail streamers soaring.

Daisy looks up.

She looks to where
the kite line is coming from.

She runs towards it.

Up the hill, down the hill,
across the field to the big house
at the edge of town.

William is in the garden
at the front of the house.
He is holding the kite's
spool of string.

Daisy watches through
the fence.

He opens the gate, "Hello," he says.
"I'm William."

He hands Daisy the spool.
The kite tugs and pulls.
Daisy laughs.

William shows her
how to steer the kite.
It swishes and swirls,
dives and zooms.

He shows Daisy how
to bring the kite closer.
It flitters and flutters.

He shows her how
to send it up high.
The kite soars and wheels.

Daisy runs with the kite.

She runs through the gate,
across the field, up the hill
and down the hill,
watching the kite dance
through the sky all the way.

She does not look back once.

At home she puts
the kite away.
She puts it where
no one will find it.

Daisy looks at the kite every day
but she does not fly it.

Until one day she can wait no more.

She takes the kite to the hill.
She lets out some line and runs.
When she feels the kite
catch the breeze, she releases it.

Up and away.

She sees William watching.

He looks at her for one moment.
Then he turns and walks away.

Daisy keeps flying the kite.
It pulls hard away from her.
She yanks it back.
It crashes to the ground.

Daisy takes the kite
home. She puts it back
in its hiding place.

She lies awake all night.

When the sun comes up,
Daisy takes the kite
out of its hiding place.
She runs to the big house.

There is no one in the garden.

She rests the kite against
the mailbox. Then she
picks up a stick and writes
in the sand on the path.

She walks back across the field and
up the hill and down the hill.

That afternoon there is something
fluttering in the sky. It is yellow.
It is coming over the hill towards her.

William is holding the spool.
He is carrying a box.

He sits down beside Daisy and opens the box.
He pulls out some paper and glue,
some ribbon and line.

"Which color?" he asks.
Daisy points at the red.

William measures and cuts.
Daisy stretches and pastes and ties.
Together, they make a new kite.

Then they run to the hill.

Blue sky, yellow kite, red kite dancing.

In memory of Buhle, who loved her yellow kite —JAH

For Ruby —JB

Text copyright © Janet A. Holmes 2016

Illustrations copyright © Jonathan Bentley 2016

First published in Australia in 2016 by Little Hare Books (an imprint of Hardie Grant Egmont)

Original edits by Margrete Lamond and Alyson O'Brien;
original production management by Sally Davis; and original design by Vida & Luke Kelly.

First published in the U.S.A. in 2017 by Peter Pauper Press, Inc.

Published by Peter Pauper Press, Inc.
202 Mamaroneck Avenue
White Plains, New York 10601 U.S.A.

Library of Congress Cataloging-in-Publication Data Available

ISBN 978-1-4413-2482-5

Manufactured for Peter Pauper Press, Inc.

Produced by Pica Digital, Singapore

Printed through Asia Pacific Offset

Printed in Shenzhen, Guangdong Province, China

7 6 5 4 3 2 1

Visit us at www.peterpauper.com

*The illustrations in this book were created using pencil and watercolor,
and the various elements were put together using Photoshop.*

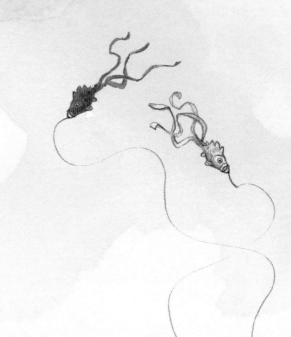